REDEMPTION

Start Publishing PD is a registered trademark of Start Publishing PD LLC
Manufactured in the United States of America

Cover art: Shutterstock/Taisiya Kozorez

Cover design: Jennifer Do

10 9 8 7 6 5 4 3 2 1

ISBN 979-8-8809-1059-5

REDEMPTION

Robert F. Young

They called him "The Jet-propelled Dutchman," but he was neither Dutch nor jet-propelled. He was neo-Terran. In common with all interplanetary spaceships of his day, his ship employed the Lamarre displacement-drive. His name was Nathaniel Drake.

Legend has it that whenever he put into port he searched for a certain woman in the hope of redeeming himself through love, but the makers of legends are—prone to draw parallels where no true parallels exist. Nathaniel Drake searched for a certain woman yes; but the woman for whom he searched was even more of a ghost than he was, and it was not love through which he hoped to redeem himself, but hate.

His story begins in a region of space off the orbital shores of Iago Iago, not long after the "Suez Canal" sprang its first "leak." In those days, the Sirian Satrapy was at the height of her industrial career. Her globular merchant ships busily plied her interplanetary seas, and her Suez Canal freighters left Way-out. almost daily for the ravenous marts of Earth. Her planets prospered and her peoples dwelled in peace and plenty and her politicians lived high on the hog. Only one of her ten ecosphere worlds knew not the blessings of civilization. This one—Iago Iaga—had been set aside for displaced indigenes in accordance with section 5, paragraph B-81, of the Interstellar Code, and was out of bounds to poet and pillager alike.

Nathaniel Drake was transporting a cargo of pastelsilk from Forget Me Not to Dior. Forget Me Not and Dior, as any schoolboy will tell you, are Sirius VIII and X respectively. Between their orbits lies the orbit of Sirius IX, or Iago Iago. Now at the time of Drake's run, these three planets were in conjunction, and consequently, in order to avoid the gravitic pull of Iago Iago, he had programmed the automatic pilot to swing the one-man ship into a wide detour. Although he did not know it at the time, this detour had already brought the *Fly by Night* into an area of space seldom "trodden by the foot of man."

When the "Suez Canal warp-process" proved impracticable for interplanetary runs, inter-planetary spacemen accepted their lot once and for all and adopted three standard measures to combat solitude. In the order of their importance, these measures were (1) girlie reali-tapes, (2) girlie stereo-comics, and (3) hangoverless gin. Nathaniel Drake had nothing against

5

watered-down voyeurism, but he believed in slaking a thirst, not in tantalizing it; hence during most of his runs he concentrated on measure number three—*i.e.*, hangoverless gin. The present run was no exception, and he was in the middle of his fifth fifth when the knock sounded on his cabin door.

*

He was not a man who took fright easily, and he never panicked. He finished filling the glass he had just emptied, and set the bottle back down on the chart table. He could hear the faint creaking of the hull re-enforcing beams and the subdued murmuring of the grav generator in the power room below him. For a while, there were no other sounds. Then the knock came again.

Deliberately Drake got up, removed his ion gun from the rack above his bunk, and laid it on the table. He sat back down again. "Come in," he said.

The door opened, and a girl entered.

She was quite tall. Her hair was light-brown, and her brown eyes were set wide-apart in a thin, rather high-cheek-boned face. They were strange eyes. They seemed to be looking both outward and inward at the same time. Atop her head sat a small kepi, its hue strictly in keeping with the blue-grayness of her coat-blouse and skirt. Army of the Church of the Emancipation uniforms were noted for their severity, and hers was no exception. In her case, however, the severity seemed to have been lost in the shuffle, and catching the sweep of her thighs as she moved into the room, Drake guessed why. She was stacked, this girl was stacked so stunningly that the fact would have been self-evident even if she bad been wearing a blanket.

The thoroughness of his scrutiny neither escaped nor disconcerted her. She did seem somewhat taken aback by his appearance, however. Small wonder: he needed a haircut, and the sideburns and chin whiskers that symbolized his captaincy had spread out into an unkempt beard that made him look fifty years of age instead of the thirty-two he actually was. "I-I imagine you're surprised to see me," she said.

Her voice was husky, but rich and full, and lent her words a resonance that words seldom get to know. Drake dug up another glass, poured it half full of gin and offered it to her. She declined it, as he had known she would. "No thank you," she said.

He drank the gin himself, then sat back in his chair and waited. While waiting, he pondered the why and the whereby of her presence. The whereby gave him no trouble: the starboard storeroom provided sufficient space for a penurious passenger to stowaway, and venality was certainly a common enough ailment among port officials. The why, however, was a horse of a different dimension.

She tethered it herself. "I want you to put me down on Iago Iago," she said. "I'll pay you—pay you well. It would have been impractical for me to take a passenger ship—with so many witnesses, the pilot wouldn't have dared to land me. I—I gambled that a loner like yourself might. Iago rago's in conjunction now, and you won't lose more than a few hours, and no one will ever know."

He was staring at her. "Iago Iago! Why should you want me to put you down in Iago Iago?"

"The Polysirians are expecting the resurrection of their supreme saint. I—I want to be on hand to witness it."

"Nonsense!" Drake said. "When you're dead, you're dead, and that goes for saints and sinners alike."

Golden flecks danced briefly in her brown eyes. "Does it, Mr. Drake? Then how do you explain the Potomac Peregrination?"

"I don't have to explain it because I don't believe in it. But to get back to specifics: even assuming that there *is* a resurrection about to take place on Iago Iago, there would be no way for the news to have reached you."

"We have ways. Call it an interplanetary grapevine, if you like. The supreme saint Prophesied that he would rise from the dead before the passing of a single year and appear in the heavens for all to see, and then descend among the people."

To gain time for reflection, Drake dropped the subject and asked her name. "Annabelle," she said. "Saint Annabelle Leigh."

"And how old are you?"

"Twenty-three. Please put me down on Iago Iago, Mr. Drake."

"You. said you were prepared to pay. How much?"

She turned her back on him, did something to her coat-blouse, and swung around a moment later with a money belt in her hands. She held it out to him. "It contains two thousand credits. Count them, if you like."

He shook his head. "Put it back on. I wouldn't risk losing my pilot's license for ten times that amount."

"But there *isn't* any risk. I'm certainly not going to tell anyone that you violated the code."

He regarded her speculatively. "Credits aren't the only form of negotiable cash," he said.

She did not even blush. "I am prepared to pay in that kind of cash too."

He was dumbfounded. Sex was not forbidden to Church of the Emancipation girls, but usually at the merest hint of it they ran away and hid somewhere. For a moment, remembering the sweep of her thighs when she had entered the room, he was tempted; but only for a moment. Recovering himself, he said, "I'm afraid that kind of cash won't suffice either. My pilot's license is my bread and butter, and I value my, bread and butter highly." He stood up. "In my capacity as captain of this vessel I hereby place you under arrest and order you to return to your self-chosen quarters and to remain there for the duration of this voyage."

Disbelief darkened her wide-apart brown eyes. Then golden motes of anger came and chased the darkness away. She made a wild grab for the ion gun on the table. He thwarted her easily, seized her arm and, towering above her, escorted her out of the cabin and down the companionway to the starboard storeroom. The starboard storeroom adjoined the hull, and in common with all hull compartments, it was equipped with a lock instead of a door. After shoving Saint Annabelle Leigh inside, he adjusted the sealing mechanism so that the lock could be opened only from the outside, then he turned to go.

She ran forward and caught his arm. There was desperation in her brown eyes. "*Please* put me down on Iago Iago."

He freed his arm, stepped out into the corridor, and closed the lock behind him.

An hour later, his ship passed through a Lambda-Xi field.

At least Drake thought it was a Lambda-Xi field. Certainly its effect upon himself and the *Fly by Night* fitted the hypothetical description given in section 3, chapter 9 of *The Pilot's Handbook* a prose-work which all spacemen were required to know by heart. The bulkheads "shimmered"; the artificial atmosphere took on a "haze-like aspect"; the deck "desolidified." As for

Drake himself, he experienced a "painful prickling of nerve-ends and a slight vertigo." Then translucence—"the prelude to total disintegration" came to ship and master alike.

The handbook went on to state that in view of the fact that no one had ever passed through a Lambda-Xi field and survived, all knowledge pertaining to the preliminary effects of such a passage had had to be extrapolated. It then added reassuringly that since such fields were exceedingly rare, the danger they represented was virtually negligible. The handbook said nothing, however, about any handwriting on the wall. Handwriting there was, though, just the same. Standing in his ship, through the translucent bulkheads and hull of which he could make out the stars, Drake read the single word:

DEATH.

And yet death did not come. Neither did total disintegration—if a distinction can be drawn. The *Fly by Night* went right on being translucent, and so did Nathaniel Drake.

He took a tentative step. He took another. The deck supported him, even though he could look down through it and through the decks beneath it and through the hull and dimly see the stars yes, and in the nearer distance, the green globe of Iago Iago. He raised his hand and, and found that he could see through his flesh too. He got a mirror and hung it on the wall and stared into his translucent face. He could see right through his reflected eyes to the reflected wall behind him. He could see right through his reflected cheeks and chin. Looking down at himself, he found that he could see through his body. Through his clothes. The translucence was such that the combination of clothes and flesh cancelled out nakedness; nevertheless, his spaceshoes and his spaceslacks and his thigh-length spacecoat were as unquestionably spectral as he was.

And yet he felt whole. His body had solidity. He lived and breathed. His ghostly ship still sped on its way to the distant shores of Dior. Maybe he was dead, but he did not feel dead: I think, therefore I am . . .

He got out the log and set down the co-ordinates of the field. Abruptly he remembered his passenger, and ran down the companionway to the starboard storeroom. However, he did not throw open the lock. If he had he really would have been dead. Beyond the translucent bulkhead lay the utter airlessness of space. The storeroom was gone. So were all the other starboard compartments. So was the starboard hull.

So was Saint Annabelle Leigh.

*

Nathaniel Drake sought out Madame Gin, only to find that she too was a ghost of her former self. Nevertheless, she had not lost her sixty-proof personality, and he consulted her at considerable length—throughout the rest of the voyage. in fact—beseeching her to close up the rather raw wound that had appeared in the side of , his hitherto impregnable conscience. This, Madame Gin obstinately refused to do.

Between consultation he put his mind to work on a pair of pressing problems. The first problem had to do with his cargo. It had come through, every yard of it, but it had come through the way the ship itself had come through—with the exception, Of course, of the starboard side, which had apparently passed through the center of the field and been disintegrated altogether. It was ironic that a vessel so effective when it came to nullifying theremo-nuclear devices could be so utterly helpless against Lambda-Xi bombardment. Translucent to begin with, the pastelsilk was now virtually transparent and undoubtedly would be rejected by *Dernier Cri* Garments, the New Paris firm that had ordered it. Worse, he was bonded for it, and if the bonding company had to stand the entire loss, his ship would have to be forfeited, and his career as an independent merchant spaceman would be over.

The second problem had to do with his ghosthood. He did not have to ask himself how people would react to his appearance because he knew how he himself reacted to it whenever he looked into the mirror. And it was no good arguing that the mirror was a ghost of its former self too. He had merely to glance down at his hands to prove that the degree of emphasis was negligible.

Invariably his thoughts reverted to the wound in his conscience, whereupon he would rejoin Madame Gin at the chart table. Oh, he had a hundred arguments in his favor. He had not asked Saint Annabelle Leigh to stowaway on his ship, had he? He had not known that the ship was going to undergo Lambda-Xi bombardment, had he? He had not known that the starboard section was doomed, had he? But, while each question could be answered with a resounding "no," the cold cruel truth marched inexorably on: If he had acceded to Annabelle Leigh's request and put in for Iago Iago, she would still be alive, and by not acceding to her request and by locking her in the starboard storeroom, he had afforded Fate a very large assist.

"I wash my hands of it," he told Madame Gin. "I'm no more to blame for her death than Pilate was to blame for the death of Christ the First."

Madame Gin was silent.

"It's not my fault she was a saint," he said, "That's what makes it seem worse than it really is—her being a saint, I mean."

Madame Gin said nothing.

"If she hadn't been a saint, it wouldn't be half so bad," Drake went on. "If she'd been some bum peddling her posterior, it probably wouldn't bother me at all. Why the hell should I care just because she was a saint? It's crazy, I tell you. Hell, she wasn't even a good saint. Good saints don't go around making the kind of proposition she made me, no matter what the cause. Saint Annabelle Leigh isn't quite as noble as you might think."

"Wasn't," said Madame Gin.

"All right then, I killed her . . I'll even admit it. All I'm trying to say is that her being a saint makes it worse."

"Murderer," said Madame Gin.

Nathaniel Drake seized her around the neck, whereupon she turned into an empty bottle. He smashed the bottle on the edge of the table, and spectral splinters flew in all directions. "I'm not a murderer!" he screamed. "I'm not, I'm not, I'm not."

*

The first person to set eyes on "The Jet-propelled Dutch-man" was the pilot of the New Paris sewage barge. He saw the ghost ship rather than its ghostly occupant, but this is of small consequence in view of the fact that the same looseness of terminology that marks the original legend also marks the second. He took one long look, then dumped his cargo into orbit posthaste and put back into port. The word spread rapidly, and when Nathaniel Drake put down some fifteen minutes later the New Paris streets and rooftops were jammed with jaded curiosity seekers hopefully waiting to be scared out of their wits. They were not disappointed.

REDEMPTION

It is one thing to scare people who have no chestnuts in the fire that frightens them; it is quite another to scare people who have. The *Fly by Night* had barely settled itself on its anti-grav jacks when a ground car came skimming across the spacestrip and drew up before the cargo dock. Out of the car stepped Thaddeus P. Terringer, president of *Dernier Cri* Garments, Dorrel Numan, vice president of *Dernier Cri* Garments, and the mayor of New Paris, who had his finger in the pie a la mode somewhere but exactly where not even the IRS troopers had been able to find out. Nathaniel Drake did not keep his visitors waiting, but donned his anti-grav belt, opened the ventral lock, and came drifting down to the dock. He had not shaved in two weeks, his unkempt hair hung over his forehead, and he was as translucent as tissue paper. They gaped,

The dock, rising as it did some five feet above the spacestrip, gave him an eminence of sorts, and the eminence, in turn, gave him confidence. "First time I ever rated a welcoming party," he said. "Where's the red carpet?"

Thaddeus P. Terringer was the first of the tongue-tied trio to recover his voice. He was a tall portly man, and he was attired as were his companions in the latest of *Dernier Cri* Garments' creations for the modern male: a pink tophat, a green, form-fitting suit of hand-twilled *thrip* fuzz, and high-heeled plastigator shoes. "Drake," he said, "you're drunk."

"No I'm not—I'm disintegrated."

Terringer took a backward step. So did Dorrel Numan and the mayor. "You went through a Lambda-Xi field!" Numan exclaimed.

"That's about the size of it."

"Nonsense," Terringer said.

"No one could survive LambdaXi bombardment."

"You call this survival?" Drake asked.

"The cargo," groaned the mayor. "What about the cargo?"

Drake answered him. "With a little luck, it might make good wrapping material for invisible bread. Put on your belt and go up and take a look."

By this time, the port master had arrived upon the scene. "I don't want anyone to board that ship till I've run a radiation check on it," he said. "Meanwhile Drake, take it up and park it on the five-hundred foot level. I

12

don't know what happened to it and I don't know what happened to you; but I'm not taking any chances."

"Bring back a sample bolt," Terringer said. "We won't be contaminated if we look at it from a distance."

Drake nodded, adjusted his belt and guided himself up through the ventral lock. He extended the anti-grav jacks to five hundred feet, then, after getting a bolt of pastelsilk out of the hold, he drifted down to the dock again. He unrolled the bolt a little ways and held it up so that Terringer, Numan and the mayor, all of whom had retreated to a safer distance, could get a good look at it. It was as tenuous as mist, and owed what little viability it still possessed to the exquisite blueness which the worms of Forget Me Not had imparted to it. Terringer groaned. So did Numan. So did the mayor. "And it's all like that?" Terringel' asked.

Drake nodded. "Every last yard."

"Take it back to Forget Me Not," Terringer said.

Drake stared at him. "Why? They won't make it good."

"Of course they won't. But they may be able to induce their worms to reprocess it, or be able to salvage it in some other way. Meanwhile, we'll just have to order another shipment." He regarded Drake shrewdly. "You'd better hope they *can* salvage it. If they can't, your bonding company will be liable, and you know what that means." He glanced skyward to where the maimed and ghostly *Fly by Night* hovered like an awry balloon. "Although how a ship in that condition can be auctioned off is beyond me."

He turned, and together with Numan and the mayor re-entered the ground car and skimmed away. Drake felt suddenly, desperately sober. "Before you run a radiation check on my ship, run one on me," he told the port master. "I'm going into town and tie a good one on."

The port master grinned sympathetically. "Will do, Mr. Drake. I'll have the doc take a look at you too."

He was as good as his word, and both the *Fly by Night* and Drake checked out satisfactorily. Drake then went to see the port doctor, who gave him a complete physical and finally confessed in a rather awed voice that he could find nothing wrong with him. Afterward, Drake visited the Port Exchange Bank, turned in his translucent credit notes for a less spectral species, and withdrew his savings—a matter of some five hundred Rockefellows. However, he did not tie a good one on. He did not tie any kind of a one on. He had barely set foot outside the port when it all began. People looked at him and ran away, or, even worse, stared at him and followed him wherever he went. The first lush lair he went into emptied almost as soon as he stepped in the door. In the next, the bartender refused to serve him. He said hello to a pretty girl walking down the street, and she fainted right before his eyes. He had gotten a haircut and a beard-trim by that time in one of the automatic barber booths scattered strategically throughout the city, but apparently neither concession to propriety had made his appearance any the less ghastly. Finally, in desperation, he visited one of New Paris' leading physicists. The physicist ran a lengthy series of tests on him, stared at him for a long time, then asked, "Are you of Dutch descent by any chance?"

"No," Drake said; and left.

He bought ten fifths of gin and returned "to his ship. It had already been recharged and reprovisioned. Repairing it of course, had been out *of* the question. He thumbed his nose at the city as he soared spaceward. Soon he was beyond the sewage belt and free among the stars.

Forget Me Not

IN Nathaniel Drake's day, the worms of Forget Me Not were legion. All over Silk City you could hear the sad susurrus of their tiny bodies as they spun their colorful cocoons in the long low sheds thoughtfully provided for them by the good folk of Pastelsilks, Inc. Toward twilight, the whispering would fade away, then, with the timid twinkling of the first star, it would come to life again and build up and up and up until the night would be one great vast whispering of worms at work—pink worms, green works, blue worms, yellow worms, spinning silk such as had never been known before and will never be known again, for now the worms of Forget Me Not are dead.

Raise one more monument to the onward march of mankind. Place it beside the statue of the buffalo. You know where the statue of the buffalo stands. It stands right next to the statue of the blue whale.

Nathaniel Drake was well acquainted with the whispering. Forget Me Not was his birthplace, and his father had brought him to the fabled city-farm when Drake was a small boy. In his capacity as merchant spaceman, Drake had been there many times since, but it was the first time that stood out the most vividly in his memory. His father had been a grower of multi-pastels, a Forget Me Not plant genus whose mulberry-like leaves formed the worms' main diet, and had occasionally come to Silk City on business. On one of these occasions he had brought the boy Nathaniel with him and taken him through several of the long low sheds, hoping that the experience might help the boy to forget about his mother, who had died the spring before and about whom he had been brooding ever since. There had been the sad susurrus of the worms working, and the glowing of colorful cocoons in the gloom, and in the processing sheds there had been the relentless turning of the automatic reels and the tiny corpses falling to the floor, one by one, and the boy Nathaniel, obsessed with thoughts of death, had wondered why more of the larvae were not spared the ignominy of the heat-treatment ovens and allowed to attain the apotheosis that was their birthright, not knowing then the senseless selfishness of mankind.

The man Nathaniel had not wondered. The man Nathaniel had not cared. The ghost of the man Nathaniel cared even less.

"Hello," said the ghost to a pretty girl as it passed her on the street.

The girl screamed, and ran away.

An old woman looked at him with horror in her eyes, then looked the other way. An IRS trooper stopped and stared.

Nathaniel Drake went on.

Behind him in the Silk City spaceport, a trio of reluctant techs from Pastelsilks, Inc. were conducting various tests upon his cargo in order to determine whether or not it could be salvaged. As their findings would have to be processed through the executive echelons of the company and would not be made a known to him till later in the day, he had a few hours to kill.

He did not intend to kill them in lush lairs, however. He had a wound to take care of.

REDEMPTION

It was the wound that had appeared in the side of his conscience. It had festered on the trip in from Dior, and now it was so painful that he could barely endure it. Madame Gin had only made it worse.

Conscience-wounds are different from physical wounds. In treating physical wounds, you attack the effect. In treating conscience-wounds, you attack the cause. Once the cause is eliminated, the wound automatically closes. This is rarely possible, but quite *often* the cause can be weakened, in which case the wound, while it will never completely close, will at least be less painful. In Nathaniel Drake's case, the cause was Saint Annabelle Leigh. If he could prove to himself that his suspicions were correct and that she had been something less than her sainthood would seem to indicate, a quantity of his pain might go away, and if he could discredit her sainthood altogether, his wound might close completely.

He proceeded directly to the local headquarters of the Army of the Church of the Emancipation. There, he inquired whether a Saint Annabelle Leigh were signed to any of the local chapels. A white-faced clerk replied in the affirmative, and referred him to the Saint Julia Ward Howe chapel on Redemption Street.

In common with all Church of the Emancipation chapels, the Saint Julia Ward Howe chapel was an unpretentious wooden building, long and narrow, with crossed Confederate and Union flags hanging above its entrance. Entering, Drake walked down a narrow aisle between two rows of backless benches and paused in front of a small pulpit upon which a crude lectern stood. Beyond the lectern there was a curtained doorway, and above this doorway two more crossed-flags hung. Presently the curtains parted, and a tall, pale man with a seamed and narrow face and gray and quiet eyes stepped onto the pulpit. Hi am Saint Andrew," he began, then stopped in staring consternation,

"I'm Nathaniel Drake, the captain of the *Fly by Night*," Drake said. "I've come about Saint Annabelle Leigh."

Comprehension supplanted the consternation on Saint Andrew's lined face—comprehension and relief. "I am so glad you came, Mr. Drake. I am but just returned from the port, where I was informed that you had just left. I—I refrained from asking them about Saint Annabelle. Tell me, is she all right?

Did you put her down on Iago Iago? I have been half out of my mind ever since I heard what happened to you and your ship."

"I had bad news for , you," Drake said. "Saint ' Annabelle Leigh is dead."

The whispering of the worms crept into the room. Saint Andrew's immaculate blue-gray uniform seemed suddenly several sizes too large for him. "Dead? Please- tell me that's not true, Mr. Drake."

"I can't," Drake said. "But I can tell you how it happened." He did so briefly. "So you can see it wasn't my fault," he concluded. "I *couldn't* put her down on Iago Iago. It would have meant jeopardizing my pilot's license, and piloting a ship is all I know how to do. It isn't fair to ask a man to put his livelihood on the block—it isn't fair at all. She should have contacted me before she stowed away. You simply *can't* hold me responsible for what happened."

"Nor do I, Mr. Drake." Saint Andrew wiped away a tear that had run halfway down his cheek. "She did what she did against my advice," he went on presently. "The information she had received concerning a resurrection on Iago Iago was of dubious origin to say the least, and I was dead set against her stowing away on board your ship in any event, but she was very set in her ways. None of which in the least alleviates the cruel fact of her death."

"She left much to be desired as a saint then?" Drake asked.

"On the contrary, she was one of the finest persons I have ever indoctrinated. One of the kindest and the gentlest. And in all my years of service in the Army of the Church of the Emancipation I have never seen a more dedicated and selfless soldier than she was. Her her passing grieves me immeasurably, Mr. Drake."

Drake looked at the floor. He felt suddenly tired. "May I sit down, Saint Andrew?" he said.

"Please do."

He sank down on the nearest bench. "Was she a native of Forget Me Not?"

"No. She came from the vineyards of Azure—from a little province called *Campagne Piasible.*" Saint Andrew sighed: "I remember vividly the first time I saw her. She was so pale and so thin. And her eyes—I have never seen torture in anyone's eyes that could compare to the torture I saw in hers. She walked in here one morning, much in the same way you yourself walked in, and she knelt down before the lectern and when I appeared, she said, 'I want to die.' I stepped down from the pulpit and raised her to her feet. "No, child,' I said, 'you do not want to die, you want to serve—else you would not have come here,' and it was then that she lifted up her eyes and I saw the torture in them. In the two years that followed, much of the torture went away, but I knew somehow that all of it never would." Saint Andrew paused. Then, "There was a quality about her which I cannot quite describe, Mr. Drake. It was in the way she walked. In the way she talked. Most of all, it manifested itself when she stood up here behind the lectern and spread the Word. Would you like to hear one of her sermons? I taped them—everyone."

"Why-why yes," Drake said. Saint Andrew turned, parted the curtains behind the lectern, and disappeared into the room beyond. He reappeared a few moments later, bearing an archaic tape-recorder which he placed upon the lectern. "I selected a tape at random," he said, flicking the switch. "Listen."

For a while there was no sound save the whispering of the worms, and then above the whispering came her rich, full voice. Sitting there in the dim chapel, Drake pictured her standing straight and tall behind the lectern, her stern, blue-gray uniform trying vainly to tone down the burgeoning of her breasts and the thrilling sweep of her calves and thighs; her voice rising now in rich and stirring resonance and filling the room with unpremeditated beauty . . .

"I have chosen to speak to you this day of the Potomac Peregrination, of the walking of His ghost upon the land; of the rising of His stone figure from the ruins of the temple where it had sat in silent meditation for three score and seventeen years, and of its coming to life to walk down to the blood-red sea, there to fall asunder on the beach. They will tell you, No, this did not happen, that the broken statue was borne there by men who wished to immortalize Him, and they will supply you with pseudo-scientific data that will seem to prove that the Planet of Peace that hovered above His head and then came down and absorbed His ghost and bore it from the face of the earth was no more than a mass-figment in the minds of the beholders. Yes, they will tell you this, these cynical-minded people will, these fact-stuffed creatures who are incapable of believing that a man can become immortal, that stone can transcend stone; that this kindest of men was the strongest of men and the greatest of men and the most enduring of men, and walks like a giant in our midst even unto this day. Well let it be known by all present, and let it be bruited about, that *I* believe: *I* believe that stone can take on life and that this great man *did* rise from the ruins of His desecrated temple to walk upon the land; like a towering giant He walked, a giant with the fires of righteousness burning in His eyes, and He did raise His voice against the bombs falling and He did wipe the incandescence from the hellish heavens with His terrible gaze, and the thunder of His tread did set the very earth to trembling as He walked down the Potomac to the sea, 'Lo, I have arisen,' He proclaimed. 'Lo, I walk again! Look at Me, ye peoples of the earth—I have come to emancipate you from your shackling fears, and I have summoned the Planet of Peace from out of the immensities of space and time to transport My ghost to the stars. Lo, I *force* peace upon you, ye peoples of the earth, and I command you to remember always this terrible day when you drove Kindness from your doorsteps and threw wide your portals to Perdition . . . ' Yes, He said these things, I swear unto you He said them as he walked down the Potomac to the sea beneath the brief bright bonfires of the bombs, the Planet of Peace shining high above His head, and if you cannot believe in the walking of His ghost upon the land and in His ascension to the stars, then you are as one dead, without hope, without love, without pity, with out kindness, without humanity, without humility, without sorrow, without pain, without happiness, and without life. Amen."

The sad susurrus of the worms crept softly back into the room. With a start, Drake realized that he had bowed his head.

He raised it abruptly. Saint Andrew was regarding him with puzzled eyes. "Have you notified her family, Mr. Drake?"

"No," Drake said. "I mentioned the matter to no one."

"I'll radio them at once then, and tell them everything." Saint Andrew rewound the tape, removed it from the recorder, and started to slip it into his pocket. "Wait," Drake said, getting to his feet.

Again, the puzzled regard. "Yes ?"

"I'd like to buy it," Drake said. "I'll pay you whatever you think it's worth."

REDEMPTION

Saint Andrew stepped down from the pulpit and handed him the tape. "Please accept it as a gift. I'm sure she would have wanted you to have it." There was a pause. Then, "Are you a believer, Mr. Drake?"

Drake pocketed the tape. "No. Oh, I believe that the War of Nineteen Ninety-nine came to a halt on the very day it began all right. What I don't believe is that the nuclei of the enemy warheads were negated by the 'terrible gaze' of a second Christ. I've always gone along with the theory that they were negated by the bombardment of a Lambda Xi field that 'slipped its moorings' and wandered into the area—the same kind of a bombardment that nearly negated me."

"And a commendable theory it is too—but basically isn't it as dependent upon divine intervention as the Potomac Peregrination?"

"Not necessarily. Such concurrences seem providential merely because we try to interpret the macrocosm on a microcosmic scale. Well, I have , to be on my way, Saint Andrew. The powers-that-be at Pastelsilks should have come to some decision concerning my transparent cargo by this time. Thank you for the tape, and for your trouble."

"Thank *you* for bringing me news of Saint Annabelle, Mr. Drake. Even though it was bad. Goodbye."

"Goodbye," Drake said, and left.

*

The offices of Pastelsilks, Inc. were as many as they were magnificent, and the building that houses them pre-empted almost an entire acre. The whispering of the worms was absent here, shut out by sound-proof construction or devoured by the sterile humming of air-conditioning units. "Right this way, Mr. Drake," a frightened office girl said. "Mr. Pompton is waiting for you."

The vice president of Pastelsilks, Inc. gave a start when Drake entered, but Drake was accustomed by this time to the reactions his appearance gave rise to and no longer paid them any heed. "Good news or bad news, Mr. Pompton?" he said.

"Bad news, I'm afraid. Please sit down, Mr. Drake."

Drake did so. "But surely my cargo must be worth something."

20

"Not to us, it isn't. Nor to *Dernier Cri* Garments. And there's no way it can be salvaged. But you just might be able to dispose of it on one of the more backward planets, and to this end Pastelsilks, Incorporated is willing to defer demanding restitution from your bonding company for six months."

"Six months doesn't give me very much time to peddle a thousand bolts of invisible silk," Drake said.

"*I consider it a very handsome* gesture on our part. Of course if you're not interested, we can—"

"I'll give it a try," Drake said. "Which of the backward planets would you recommend?"

"Marie Elena, Dandelion, Little Sun, Dread—"

"Is Azure a possibility?"

"Why yes, Azure ought to provide a potential market. Its peoples are largely members of the peasantry, and it's conceivable that they might be attracted by bolts of colored mists and pastel nothingness."

"Good," Drake said, getting to his feet. "I'll be on my way then."

"One minute, Mr. Drake. Before you leave, I would like to make a suggestion with regard to your appearance."

Drake frowned. "I don't see what I can do about it."

"There are quite a number of things you can do about it. First of all, you can buy yourself some clothing that is *not* translucent. Secondly, you can buy yourself a pair of skin-tight gloves. Thirdly, you can buy yourself a flesh-colored rubber mask that will align itself to your features. You can, in other words, cease being an apparition in the eyes of everyone you meet, and become a perfectly presentable silk salesman."

Drake shifted his weight from fine foot to the other. "I'm afraid I can't do any of those things," he said.

"You can't? In the name of all that's wholesale, why not?"

The word "penance" came into Drake's mind, but he ignored it. "I don't know," he said. He turned to go.

"One more minute please, Mr. Drake, will you enlighten me on a little matter before you leave?"

"All right."

REDEMPTION

Mr. Pompton cleared his throat. "Are you of Dutch descent by any chance?"

"No," Drake said, and left.

Azure

The best way to build a mental picture of Azure is to begin with a bunch of grapes. The bunch of grapes is cobalt-blue in hue and it is part of a cobalt-blue cluster of similar bunches. The cluster hangs upon a vine which is bursting with heart-shaped leaves, and the vine is one of many similar vines that form a verdant row, in turn, is one of many similar rows that form a verdant vineyard. You see them now, do you not?—these lovely vineyards rolling away, and the white, red-roofed houses in between?—the intervals of green and growing fields in the blue swaths of rivers and the sparkling zigzags of little streams?—the blue eyes of little lakes looking up into the warm blue sky where big Sirius blazes and little Sirius beams? Now, picture people working. in the fields and in the vineyards; picture trees, and children playing underneath them; picture housewives coming out back doors and shaking homemade rugs that look like little rainbows; picture toy-like trains humming over anti-grav beds from town to town, from city to city, tying in the entire enchanting scheme of things with the spaceport at *Vin Bleu*. Finally, picture a narrow road winding among the vineyards, and a man walking along it. A man? No, not a man-a ghost. A tall gaunt ghost in spectral space-clothes. A ghost named Nathaniel Drake.

He had come many miles by train and he had visited many towns along the way and talked with many merchants, and each time he had unfolded the sample of pastelsilk he carried and held it up for inspection, and each time the word had been no. In the town he had just left, the word had been no too, and he knew by now that wherever he went on Azure the word would be no also, but right now he did not care. Right now he was about to carry out the ulterior purpose of his visit, and the ulterior purpose of his visit had nothing to do with the selling of silk.

He could see the house already. It sat well back from the road. In it, she had grown up. Along this very road, she had walked to school. Between these verdant vineyards. Beneath this benign blue sky. Sometimes during those green years she must have sinned.

Like all its neighbors, the house was white, its roof red-tiled. In the middle of its front yard grew a Tree of Love, and the tree was in blossom. Soon now, the blossoms would be falling, for autumn was on hand. Already the time for the harvesting of the grapes had come. Had she picked in these very vineyards? he wondered. Clad in colorful clothing, had she walked along these growing banks of green and heaped baskets with brilliant blue? And had she come home evenings to this little white house and drenched her face with cool water from that archaic well over there, and then gone inside and broken bread? And afterward had she come outside and waited in the deepening darkness for her lover to appear? Nathaniel Drake's pulse-beat quickened as he turned into the path that led across the lawn to the small front porch. No matter what Saint Andrew had said, Saint Annabelle Leigh could not possibly have been all saint.

A girl in a yellow maternity dress answered the door. "She had hyacinth hair, blue eyes and delicate features. She gasped when she saw Drake, and stepped back. "I've come about Annabelle Leigh," he said quickly. "Did Saint Andrew radio you about what happened? He, said he would. I'm Nathaniel Drake."

The girl's fright departed as quickly as it bad come. "Yes; he did. Please come in, Mr. Drake. I'm Penelope Leigh-Annabelle's sister-in-law."

The room into which he stepped was both pleasant and provincial. A long wooden table stood before a big stone fireplace. There were cushioned chairs and benches, and upon the floor lay a homemade hook-rug that embodied all the colors of the spectrum. A big painting of the Potomac Peregrination hung above the mantel. The marble figure of the Emancipator had been huge to begin with, but over the centuries the minds of men had magnified it into a colossus. Artists were prone to reflect the popular conception, and the artist who had painted the present picture was no exception. In juxtaposition to the towering figure that strode along its banks, the Potomac was little more than a pale trickle; houses were matchboxes, and trees, blades of grass. Stars swirled around the gaunt gray face, and some of the stars were glowing Komets and Golems and T-4A's re-entering the atmosphere, and some of them were interceptors blazing spaceward. The sea showed blood-red in the distance, and in the background, the broken columns of the fallen Memorial were illuminated by the hellish radiance of the funeral pyre of Washington, D.C. High above the ghastly terrain hovered the pale globe of the Planet of Peace.

"Please sit down, Mr. Drake," Penelope said. "Annabelle's mother and father are in the vineyard, but they will be home soon."

Drake chose one of the cushioned chairs. "Do they hate me?" he asked.

"Of course they don't hate you, Mr. Drake. And neither do I."

"I could have averted her death, you know," Drake said. "If I'd put her down on Iago Iago as she asked me to, she would still be alive today. But I valued my pilot's license too highly. I thought too much of my daily bread."

Penelope had sat down in a cushioned chair that faced his own. Now she leaned forward, her blue eyes full upon him. "There's no need for you to justify your action to me, Mr. Drake. My husband is a Suez Canal tech, and he can't pursue his profession without a license either. He worked very hard to get it, and he wouldn't dream of jeopardizing it. Neither would I."

"That would be Annabelle's brother, wouldn't it. Is he here now?"

"No. He's on Wayout, working on the 'leak.' I say 'working on it,' but actually they haven't found it yet. All they know is that it's on the Wayout end of the warp. It's really quite a serious situation, Mr. Drake—much more serious than the officials let on. Warp seepages are something new, and very little is known about them, and Ralph says that this one could very well throw the continuum into a state of imbalance if it isn't checked in time."

Drake hadn't come all the way to *Campagne Paisible* to talk about warp seepages. "How well did you know your sister-in-law, Miss Leigh?" he asked.

"I thought I knew her very well. We grew up together, went to school together, and were the very best of friends. I *should* have known her very well."

"Tell me about her," Drake said.

She wasn't at all an outward person, and yet everyone liked her. She. was an excellent student—excelled in everything except Ancient Lit. She never said much, but when she did say something, you listened. There was something about her voice."

"I know," Drake said.

"As I said, I , *should* have known her very well, but apparently I didn't. Apparently no one else did either. We were utterly astonished when she ran away—especially Estevan Foursons."

"Estevan Foursons?"

"He's a Polysirian he lives on the next farm. He and Annabelle were to be married. And then, as I said, she ran away. None of us heard from her for a whole year, and Estevan never heard from her at all. Leaving him without a word wasn't at all in keeping with the way she was. She Was a kind and gentle person. I don't believe he's gotten over it to this day, although he did get married several months ago. I think, though, that what astonished us even more than her running away was the news that she was studying for the sainthood. She was never in the least religious, or, if she was, she kept it a deep dark secret."

"How old was she when she left?" Drake asked.

"Almost twenty. We had a picnic the day before. Ralph and I, she and Estevan. If anything was troubling her, she certainly gave no sign of it. We had a stereo-camera, and we took pictures. She asked me to take one of her standing on a hill, and I did. It's a lovely picture—would you like to see it?"

Without waiting for his answer, she got up and left the room. A moment later she returned carrying a small stereo-snapshot. She handed it to him. The hill was a high one, and Annabelle was outlined sharply against a vivid azure backdrop. She was wearing a red dress that barely reached her knees and which let the superb turn of her calves and thighs come through without restraint. Her waist was narrow, and the width of her hips was in perfect harmony with the width of her shoulders—details which her Church of the Emancipation uniform had suppressed. Spring sunlight had bleached her hair to a tawny yellow and had turned her skin golden. At her feet, vineyards showed, and the vineyards were in blossom, and it was as though she too were a part of the forthcoming harvest, ripening under the warm sun and waiting to be savored.

There was a knot of pain in Drake's throat. He raised his eyes to Penelope's. Why did you have to show me this? he asked in silent desperation. Aloud, he said, "May I have it?"

The surprise that showed upon her face tinged her voice. "Why—why yes, I suppose so. I have the negative and can get another made . . . . Did you know her very well, Mr. Drake?"

He slipped the stereo-snapshot into the inside breast-pocket of his long-coat, where it made a dark rectangle over his heart. "No," he said. "I did not know her at all."

*

Toward twilight, Annabelle's parents came in from the vineyard. The mother, buxom of build and rosy of cheek, was attractive in her own right, but she was a far cry from her daughter. In order to see Annabelle, you had to look into the father's sensitive face. You could glimpse her in the line of cheek and chin, and in the high, wide forehead. You could see her vividly in the deep brown eyes. Drake looked away.

He was invited to share the evening meal, and he accepted. However, he knew that he would not find what he was searching for here, that if there had been another side of Annabelle she had kept it hidden from her family.

Estevan Foursons was the logical person to whom to take his inquiries, and after the meal, Drake thanked the Leighs for their hospitality, said good by, and set off down the road.

Estevan Foursons lived in a house very much like the Leighs. Vineyards grew behind it, vineyards grew on either side of it, and across the road, more vineyards grew. The sweet smell of grapes ripening on the vine was almost cloying. Drake climbed the steps of the front porch, stood in the artificial light streaming through the window in the door, and knocked. A tall young man wearing pastel slacks and a red-plaid peasant blouse came down the hall. He had dark-brown hair, gray eyes, and rather full lips. Only the mahogany cast of his skin betrayed his racial origin-that, and his unruffled calm when he opened the door and saw Drake. "What do you want?" he asked.

"Estevan Foursons?"

The young man nodded.

"I'd like to talk to you about Annabelle Leigh," Drake went on "It was on my ship that she—"

"I know," Estevan interrupted. "Penelope told me. Nathaniel Drake, is it not?"

"Yes. I—"

"Why are you interested in a dead woman?"

For a moment, Drake was disconcerted. Then, "I—I feel responsible for her death in a way."

"And you think that knowing more about her will make you feel less responsible?"

"It might. Will you tell me about her?"

Estevan sighed. "I sometimes wonder if I really knew her myself. But come, I will tell you what I thought I knew. We will walk down the road—this is not for my wife's ears."

Beneath the stars, Drake said, "I talked with the saint who indoctrinated her. He thought very highly of her."

"He could hardly have thought otherwise."

Estevan turned off the road and started walking between two starlit rows of grapevines. Disappointed, Drake followed. Had Annabelle Leigh never done anything wrong? It would seem that she had not.

For some time the two men walked in silence, then Estevan said, "I wanted you to see this place. She used to come here often."

They had emerged from the vineyard and were climbing a small slope. At the top of it, Estevan paused, and Drake paused beside him. At their feet, the ground fell gradually away to the wooded shore of a small lake. "She used to' swim there naked in the starlight," Estevan said. "Often I came here to watch her, but I never let on that I knew. Come."

Heartened, Drake followed the Polysirian down the slope and through the trees to the water's edge. Drake knelt, and felt the water. It was ice-cold. A granite outcropping caught his eye. Nature had so shaped it that it brought to mind a stone bench, and approaching it more closely; he saw that someone had sculptured it into an even greater semblance. "I did that," Estevan said from behind him. "Shall we sit down?"

Seated, Drake said, "I find it difficult to picture her here. I suppose that's because I associate saints with Cold corridors and cramped little rooms. There's something pagan about this place."

Estevan did not seem to hear him. "We would bring our lunch here from the vineyards sometimes," he said. "We would sit here on this bench and eat

27

and talk. We were very much in love—at least everybody said we were. Certainly, I was. Her, I don't know."

"But she must have loved you. You were going to be married, weren't you?"

"Yes, we were going to be married." Estevan was silent for a while; then, "But I don't think she loved me. I think she was afraid to love me. Afraid to love anyone. Once, it hurt me even to think like this. Now, it is all past. I am married now, and I love my wife. Annabelle Leigh is a part of yesterday, and yesterday is gone. I can think now of the moments we spent together, and the moments no longer bring pain. I can think of us working together in the vineyards, tending the vines, and I can think of her standing in the sun at harvest time, her arms filled with blue clusters of grapes and the sunlight spilling goldenly down upon her. I can think of the afternoon we were rained out, and of how we ran through the rows of vines, the rain drenching us, and of the fire we built in the basket shed so that she could dry her hair. I can think of her leaning over the flames, her rain-dark hair slowly lightening to bronze, and I can think of the raindrops disappearing one by one from her glowing face. I can think of how I seized her suddenly in my arms and kissed her, and of how she broke wildly free and ran out into the rain, and the rain pouring down around her as she ran. I did not even try to catch her, because I knew it would do no good, and I stood there by the fire, miserable and alone, till the rain stopped, and then went home. I thought she would be angry with me the next day, but she was not. She acted as though the rain had never been, as though my passion had never broken free. That night, I asked her to marry me. I could not believe it when she said yes. No, these moments give me no more pain, and I can recount them to you with complete calm. Annabelle, I think, was born without passion, and hence could not understand it in others. She tried to imitate the actions of normal people, but there is a limit to imitation, and when she discovered this limitation she ran away."

Drake frowned in the darkness. He thought of the tape Saint Andrew had given him, of the picture that he carried in his left breast-pocket. Try as he would, he could correlate neither of the two Annabelles with the new Annabelle who had stepped upon the stage. "Tell me," he said to Estevan, "when she ran away, did you make any attempt to follow her?"

"I did not—no; but her people did. When a woman runs away because she is afraid of love, it is futile to run after her because when you catch up to her she will still be running." Estevan got to his feet. "I must be getting back—my wife will be wondering where I am. I have told you all I know."

He set off through the trees. Bitterly disappointed, Drake followed. In trying to discredit the woman he wanted to he had merely succeeded in vindicating her. The new Annabelle might be inconsistent with as for the other two, but she certainly was not inconsistent with saintliness, and as for the other two, for all their seeming disparity neither of them was inconsistent with saintliness either. It was a long step from the girl on the hill to the girl he had locked in the storeroom to die, not an illogical step, and there-fore it could be made. Two years was more than enough time to transform the surcharged fires of spring into the smoldering ones of fall— Two years?

That was the length of time she had served under Saint Andrew. In the cabin of the *Fly by Night*, however, she had given *class C. Departure time: 1901* her age as twenty-three.

The two men had reached the road. Suddenly excited, Drake turned to Estevan. "How old was she when she left?" he asked: "Exactly how old?"

"In two more months she would have been twenty."

"And when she left, did anybody check at the spaceport? Does anybody know positively that she went directly to Forget Me Not?"

"No. At the time it never occurred to anyone—not even the police—that she might have left Azure."

Then she could have gone annywhere, Drake thought. Aloud, he said, "Thank you for your trouble, Estevan. I'll be on my way."

*

He proceeded by anti-grav train to the spaceport at *Vin Bleu*, only to find that the records he desired access to were unavailable to unauthorized personnel. However, by distributing a quantity of his fast-dwindling capital (he had drawn out the second half of his bi-planetary nest egg on Forget Me Not), he managed to bring about a temporary suspension of the rule. Once handed the big departure log, he had no trouble finding the entry he wanted. It was over three years old, and read, *9 May, 3668: Annabelle Leigh via Transspacelinesto Worldwellost, class C. Departure time: 1901hours, GST.*

REDEMPTION

Hope throbbed through him. There were no Army of the Church of the Emancipation missions on Woridwellost. Worldwellost was a Mecca for sinners, not saints.

In a matter of hours, Azure was a blue blur in the *Fly by Night's* rear viewplate.

On the chart table in his cabin, Madame Gin sat. Drake regarded her for some time. For all her refusal to help him in his time of need, he still found her presence indispensable. Why, then, did he not go to her at once and enrich his intellect with her fuzzy philosophies?

Presently he shrugged, and turned away. He propped the picture Penelope had given him against the base of the chart lamp; then he incorporated the tape Saint Andrew had given him into the automatic pilot and programmed a continual series of playbacks over the intercom system. He returned to the table and sat down. Ignoring Madame Gin, he concentrated on the girl on the hill—

"I have chosen to speak to you this day of the Potomac Peregrination, of the walking of His ghost upon the land; of the rising of His stone figure from the ruins of the temple where it had sat in silent meditation for three score and seventeen years, and of its coming to life to walk down to the blood-red sea . . . "

Worldwellost

In common with Azure, Worldwellost is one of the inner planets of the vast Sirian system. However, it has little else in common with Azure, and in Nathaniel Drake's day it had even less.

Before the commercial apotheosis of its lustrous neighbor, Starbright, it had flourished as a vacation resort. Now, its once luxurious hotels and pleasure domes had fallen into desuetude, and the broad beaches for which it had once been renowned were catchalls for debris, dead fish, and decaying algae. But Worldwellost was not dead—far from it. The rottenest of logs, once turned over, reveal life at its most intense, and the rotten log of Worldwellost was no exception.

Nathaniel Drake put down in the spaceport-city of Heavenly and set forth upon his iconoclastic quest. Annabelle Leigh's trail, however, ended almost as soon as it began. She had checked into the Halcyon Hotel one day, and checked out the next, leaving no forwarding address.

Undaunted, Drake returned to the port, distributed some more of his fast-dwindling capital, and obtained access to the departure log. He found the entry presently: 26 *June, 8664: Annabelle Leigh via Transspacelines to Forget Me Not, class A. Departure time: 0619 hours, GST.*

Spacetime was synonymous with earth time and, while it was used in calculating all important time periods, such as a person's age, it seldom coincided with local calendars. Therefore, while the month and the year on Worldwellost might seem to indicate otherwise, Drake knew definitely that Annabelle Leigh had left the planet over two years ago, or approximately one year after she had arrived.

Judging from her change in travel-status, she had bettered herself, financially during that period.

Had she spent the entire year in Heavenly? he wondered. When all other attempts to obtain information about her failed, he had a photostat made of the stereo-snapshot Penelope had given him, presented it to the missing persons department of Heavenly's largest 3V station, and engaged them to flash a daily circular to the effect that he, Nathaniel Drake, would pay the sum of fifty credits to anyone providing him with bona fide information concerning the girl in the picture. He' then retired to his room at the Halcyon Hotel and waited for his visiphone to chime.

His visiphone didn't, but several days later, his door did. Opening it, he saw an old man clad in filthy rags standing in the hall. The old man took one look at him, lost what little color he had, and turned and began to run. Drake seized his arm. "Forget about the way I look," he said. "One hundred of my credits makes a Rockefellow the same as anyone else's, and I'll, pay cash if you've got the information I want."

Some of the old man's color came back. "I've got it, Mister don't you worry about that." Reaching into the inside pocket of his filthy coat, he withdrew what at first appeared to be a large map folded many times over. He unfolded it with clumsy fingers, shook it out, and held it up for Drake to see. It was a stereo-poster of a girl, life-size and in color—the same girl who had had her picture taken on a hill on Azure—

REDEMPTION

Only this time she wasn't wearing a red dress. She was wearing a *cache-sexe*, and except for a pair of slippers, that was all she was wearing.

Drake could not move.

There was a legend at the bottom of the poster. It read: *Mary Legs, now stripping at King Tutankhamen's*

Abruptly Drake came out of his state of shock. He tore the poster out of the old man's hands. "Where did you get it?" he demanded.

"I stole it. Ripped it off the , King's billboard when nobody was looking. Carried it with me ever since."

"Did you ever see her perform?"

"You bet I did! You never saw anything like it. She'd—"

"How long ago?"

"Two-three years. Big years. She's the one you want, ain't she? I knew it the minute I saw the picture on 3v. Sure, the name's different, I says to myself, but it's the same girl. You should have seen her dance, Mister. As I say, she'd—"

"Where's King Tutankhamen's place?" Drake asked.

"In Storeyville. As I say, she'd—"

"Shut up," Drake said. He counted out fifty credits and placed them in the old man's hand. The old man was regarding him intently. "You're the Jet-propelled Dutchman, ain't you."

"What if I am?"

"You don't look like a Dutchman. Are you?"

"No," Drake said, and re-entered the room and slammed the door.

*

The anti-grav trains of Worldwellost were as rundown as the towns and cities they connected. Drake rode all night and all the next morning. He didn't sleep a wink throughout the whole trip, and when he got off the train at the Storeyville station he looked even more like a ghost than he had when he had got on.

His appearance provoked the usual quota of starts and stares. Ignoring them, he made his way to the main thoroughfare. Tall and gaunt and grim, he looked up and down the two rows of grimy facades, finally spotted the neoned name he wanted, and started out. A knot of teen thieves formed behind him as he progressed down the street. "The Jet-propelled Dutchman," they cried jeeringly. "Look, the Jet-propelled Dutchman!"

He turned and glowered at them, and they ran away.

The exterior of King Tutankhamen's had a rundown mien, but it retained traces of an erstwhile elegance. Within, dimness prevailed, and Drake practically had to feel his way to the bar. Gradually, though, as the brightness of the afternoon street faded from his retina, he began to make out details. Rows of glasses; rows of bottles. Obscene paintings on the wall. A palefaced customer or two. A bartender.

Outside in the street, the teen thieves had regrouped and had taken up their jeering chant again. "The Jet-propelled Dutchman, the Jet-propelled Dutchman!" The bartender came over to where Drake was standing. He was fat, his skin was the color of nutmeg, and his hair was white. "Your-your pleasure, sir?" he said.

Eyes more perceptive now, Drake looked at the obscene paintings, wondering if she were the subject of any of them. She was not. He returned his gaze to the bartender. "Are you the owner?"

"King Tutankhamen at your service, sir. I am called 'the King'."

"Tell me about Annabelle Leigh."

"Annabelle Leigh? I know of no such person."

"Then tell me about Mary Legs."

The light that came into the King's eyes had a sublimating effect upon his face. "Mary Legs? Indeed, I can tell you about her. But tell *me* first, have you seen her lately? Tell me, is she all right?"

"She's dead," Drake said. "I killed her."

The King's fat face flattened slightly; fires flickered in his pale eyes. Then his face filled out again, and the fires faded away.

"No," he said, "she may be dead, but you did not kill her. No one would kill Mary Legs. Killing Mary Legs would be like killing the sun and the stars and the sky, and even if a man could kill these things he would not do so, and neither would he kill Mary Legs."

"I did not kill her on purpose,'" he introduced himself and told the King about the *Fly by Night's* encounter with the Lambda-Xi field, of how he had locked Saint Annabelle Leigh in the starboard storeroom to die. "If I had not been so selfish," he concluded, . "she would still be alive today."

The King looked at him pityingly. "And now your hands are bloodied, and you must seek her ghost."

"Yes," said Drake. "Now I must seek her ghost—and destroy it."

The King shook his head. "You may seek it all you want, and you may even find it. But you will never destroy it, Nathaniel Drake. It will destroy you. Knowing this, I will help you find it. Come with me."

He spoke a few words into an intercom at his elbow, then came around the bar and led the way down a spiral staircase into a subterranean room. Their entry brought vein-like ceiling lights into luminescence, and the room turned out to be a large hall. Cushioned chairs were arranged in rows on either side of a narrow ramp that protruded from a velvet-curtained stage, and to the right of the stage, a chromium piano stood.

"It is fitting that I tell you about her here," King Tutankharnen said, "for this is where she danced. Come, we will take the best seats in the house."

Drake followed him down the aisle to the juncture of stage and ramp. The King seated him m the chair nearest the juncture and took the adjacent chair for himself. Leaning back, he said, Now I will begin.

"It was over three galactic years ago when she first walked into my establishment. The tourists had not entirely forsaken Worldwellost in those days, and I was still enjoying prosperity. The bar was bright and bustling, but I saw her nevertheless the minute she stepped upon the premises. Thin, she was, and pale, and I thought at first that she was sick. When she sat down at the table by the door, I went immediately over to her side.

"'Wine, would you like ?" I asked, knowing as I do the revivifying qualities of the grape. But she shook her head. 'No,' she said, 'I want work.' 'But what can you do?' I asked. 'I can take off my clothes,' she replied. 'Is there something else I need to know?' Looking at her more closely, I saw that indeed there was nothing else she needed to know; nevertheless, there is an art of sorts to bumps and grinds, and this I told her. 'You have other girls who can show me the rudiments,' she said. 'After that, it will be up to me.' 'What is your name ?' I asked then. 'Mary Legs,' she answered. 'It is not my real name, however, and you will have to pay me in cash.' I took one more look at her, and hired her on the spot.

"It developed that she had no aptitude for bumps and grinds. It also developed that she did not need to have. The first time she danced, only a dozen men sat here in this room and watched her. The second time she danced, two dozen sat here. The next time she danced, the room was packed, the bar was overflowing, and there was a line of men waiting in the street. Some girls dance simply by walking. She was one of them. She had what is called 'poetry of motion,' but I think it was her legs, really, that most men came to see. I will let you judge for yourself. Incidentally, the piano which you will hear accompanying her was played by me."

King Tutankhamen leaned forward, slid aside a small panel just beneath the edge of the proscenium, and depressed several luminescent buttons. Instantly the lights went out, and the velvet curtains parted. A stereo-screen leaped into bright life, and a moment later, Mary Legs, *nee* Abbabelle Leigh, appeared upon it. So flawless was the illusion that it was as though she had stepped upon the stage.

Perfume reminiscent of the vineyards of Azure infiltrated the room. Drake found breathing difficult.

She was wearing a standard stripper's outfit that could be removed piece by piece. Hardly had she "appeared" upon the stage when the first piece fluttered forth and disappeared. Three more followed in swift succession. A fifth went just as she stepped, seemingly, out upon the ramp.

"She was always that way," the King whispered. "I told her that she should be coy, that she should tease, but she paid no attention. It was as though she couldn't get her clothes off fast enough."

Drake barely heard him.

Mary Legs was moving down the ramp now, and now another garment drifted forth and winked out of sight. He saw her breasts. Chords sounded in the background. A progression of ninths and elevenths. Her face was glowing; her eyes were slightly turned up. Glazed.

Drake watched the final garment disappear into the mists of time. She was down to sandals and *cache-sexe* now. Her slow walk down the ramp continued. There was poetry in the play of light upon her flesh, there was poetry in her every motion. The flabby pectorals of beauty queens, she knew not. Here was firmness; depth. Her hair burned with the yellow fires of fall, An arpeggio like the tinkling of glass chimes leaped up and formed a brief invisible halo over her head. At the base of the ramp she went through a series of contemptuous bumps and grinds, then returned casually the way she had come. Now there was a subtle difference in her walk. Sweat broke out on Drake's face. His breath burned in his throat. Eyes turned up, she saw no one, then or now; knew no one, knew nothing but the moment. Her body writhed obscenely. Notes fell around her like cool rain. Suddenly Drake realized that she had not been flaunting her sex to the audience, but to the worlds.

She began a second series of bumps and grinds. While it lacked finesse, it was obscene beyond belief, and yet, in another sense, it was somehow not obscene at all. There was something tantalizingly familiar about it, so tantalizingly familiar that he could have sworn that he had seen her dance before. And yet he knew perfectly well that he had not.

His mind ceased functioning, and he sat there helplessly, a prisoner of the moment. Presently she began a series of movements, a dance of sorts that had in it the essence of every orgy known to mankind, and yet simultaneously possessed a quality that had nothing whatsoever to do with orgies, a quality that was somehow transcendant . . . and austere. She paused transiently just above him, and her legs were graceful pillars supporting the splendid temple of her body and her head was the rising sun, then she stepped back into the screen, the lights went on, and the curtain closed.

I am a wall, and my breasts like the towers thereof:

Then as I in his eyes as: one that found peace.

It was some time before either man spoke. Then Drake said, "I'd like to buy it."

"The realitape? Why—so you can destroy it?"

"No. How much do you want?"

"You must understand;" said the King, "that it is very precious to me, that—"

"I know," Drake said. "How much?"

"Six hundred Rockefellows." The amount came perilously close to the figure to which Drake's capital had dwindled. Nevertheless, he did not haggle, but counted the hundred-credit notes out. The King removed the, realitape from the proscenium projector, and the exchange was made. "You are getting a bargain, Mr. Drake;" the King said.

"For a collector's item like that, I could get twice six hundred Rockefellows."

"When did she leave here?" Drake asked.

"About a year after she arrived. A big year. I went to her room after one of her dances and found her gone. Her clothes, everything . . . . For all her willingness to exhibit herself, she was never really one of us. She would never permit any of us to get close to her in any sense of the word. There was something tragic about her. She said once that she could not bear children, but I do not think that this had very much to do with her unhappiness. She *was* unhappy, you know, although she was very careful never to let on." The King raised his eyes, and Drake was dumfounded to see tears in them. "You have told me that after she left Worldwellost she became a saint. Somehow this does not surprise me. There is an exceedingly thin line between good and evil. Most of us manage to walk this line with a greater or lesser degree of equilibrium, but I think Mary Legs could not walk it at all: with her, I think it had to be one side or the other. Evil, she found intolerable after a while, and she ran away, crossing the line to good. But good, she eventually found intolerable too, and she ran away again. She told you that she wished to be put down on Iago Iago to witness a resurrection. This, I do not believe. Real or not the resurrection was an excuse for her. I believe that she was searching for a way of life that would combine the two extremes of good and evil and that she hoped to find it among the primitive Polysirians. And I think that she also hoped to find a man who would understand her and accept her for what she was. Do you think I may be right, Nathaniel Drake?"

"I don't know," Drake said. Abruptly he stood up. "I'll be on my way now."

King Tutankhamen touched his arm. "The question which I am about to ask is an exceedingly delicate one, Nathaniel Drake. I hope you will not take offense?"

Drake sighed wearily. "Ask it then, and get it over with."

REDEMPTION

"By any chance, are you of Dutch descent?"

"No," Drake said, and left.

*

Three of the six months which Pastelsilks, Inc. had given Drake to sell his cargo had now passed, and his cargo was undiminished by so much as a single bolt of blue. His capital, on the other hand, was virtually exhausted. Even *Der Fliegende Holländer* had never had it so bad.

Drake had not expected to be able to sell any of the pastels ilk on Worldwellost, nor, he realized in retrospect, had he expected to be able to sell any of it on Azure. It was imperative, however, that he sell it somewhere and sell it soon, for, unredeemed or not, he still intended to go on living, and in order to go on living he needed a means by which to make his daily bread, and while a ghost-ship left much to be desired, it was better than no ship at all. He had known all along that there was one place in the Sirian Satrapy where the people were naive enough to barter worthwhile goods for "bolts of blue and pastel nothingness," and that place was Iago Iago. However, he had deferred going there for two reasons. The first reason had been his eagerness to discredit Saint Annabelle Leigh, and the second had been his fear that fencing the goods he procured on Iago Iago might get him into trouble with the authorities and lead to the loss of his pilot's license. But for all his seeming success in blackening the face of the woman he wanted to hate, he had failed so completely to evoke the desired emotion that he knew by now that the cause was hopeless; and in view of the fact that his pilot's-license would be worthless if he lost his ship, the second objection was no longer valid. It had been in the books all along for him to go to Iago Iago.

He lifted up from Heavenly and found the stars again, the stars were good. Madame Gin, he left behind. After turning over the ship to the automatic pilot, he got out the realitape he had purchased from King Tutankhamen and fitted it into the girlie realitape projector. Presently Mary Legs stepped out of the past. He propped the stereos snapshot Penelope had given him against the base of the chart lamp, then he turned on the intercom. "I have chosen to speak to you this day of the Potomac Peregrination, of the walking of His ghost upon: the land," said Saint Annabelle Leigh. Mary Legs cast her final garment into the mists of time and walked lewdly down the ramp.

Perfume reminiscent of the vineyards of Azure permeated the room. Cancelling out the background music, Drake discovered that her dance blended with the words Saint Annabelle Leigh was uttering. No, not Saint Annabelle's words exactly, but the rhythm and the resonance of her voice. What the one was trying to express, the other was trying to express also. *Look at me*; they "said" in unison. *I am lonely and afraid, and full of love. Yes, yes!* cried the girl *on the hill. Full of love, full of love, full of love!* And in the cabin, vineyards blossomed, flowers bloomed; there rose a blue-bright sun, and in its radiance the boy and the girl walked, the boy Nathaniel and the girl Anna belle Leigh, and the wind blew and the grass sang and the trees put their heads together in rustling consultations . . . and all the while, the hull-beams creaked and the gray generator murmured, and the spectral *Fly by Night* sped on its way to Iago.

It was fitting that a ghost should fall in love with a ghost.

Iago. Iago.

Iago Iago is like a massive ball of yarn left lying in the hall of the universe by some capricious cosmic cat. It is emerald in hue, and when it is viewed from a great distance its atmosphere lends it a soft and fuzzy effect. This effect diminishes as the distance decreases, finally ceases to be a factor, and the planet emerges as a bright green Christmas-tree ornament hanging upon the star-bedight spruce of space.

The Polysirians were expecting Nathaniel Drake. They had been expecting him for many months. "I: will arise and come back to you, he had said. "I will appear in your sky, and come down to you, and you will know then, that His ghost did truly walk, and that it did not walk in vain." Nathaniel Drake did not know that they were expecting him, however, nor did he know that he had said these words.

He brought the *Fly by Night* down in a grassy meadow, parked it on extended anti-grav. jacks, and drifted down to the ground. He heard the shouts then, and saw the Polysirians running toward him out of a nearby forest. He would have re-boarded his ship and closed the lock behind him, but the tenor of their shouts told him that he had nothing to fear, and he remained standing in the meadow, tall and gaunt and ghostly, waiting for them to come up.

They halted a dozen yards away and formed a colorful semicircle. They wore flowers in their hair, and their sarongs and lap-laps were made of pastelsilk. The pastelsilk was decades-old. Had another trader come down out of the heavens in times past and defiled this virgin ground?

Presently the semicircle parted, and an old woman stepped into the foregound. Drake saw instantly that she was not a Polysirian. Her Church of the Emancipation uniform stood out in jarring contrast to the colorful attire of the natives, but it was not one of the mass-produced uniforms worn by her peers in the civilized sections of the satrapy. It had been spun and cut and sewn by hand, and in its very simplicity had attained a dignity that its civilized cousins could never know. Somehow he got the impression that she was wearing it for the first time.

She began walking toward him through the meadow grass. There was something tantalizingly familiar about the way she moved; something nostalgic. The brim of her kepi kept her eyes in shadow, and he could not see into them. Her cheeks were sere and thin, yet strangely lovely. She stopped before him and looked up into his face with eyes into which he still could not see. "The people of Iago Iago welcome you back, Nathaniel Drake," she said.

The heavens seemed to shimmer; the terrain took on an unreal cast. The semicircle knelt and bowed its be-flowered heads. "I don't understand," he said.

"Come with me."

He walked beside her over the meadow, the ranks of the people parting, and the people falling in behind; over the meadow and through the park-like forest and down the street of an idyllic village and up a gentle hill that swelled like a virgin's breast into the sky. The people began to sing, and the tune was a thrilling one, and the words were fine and noble.

On top of the hill lay a lonely grave. The old woman halted before it, and Drake halted beside her. Out of the corner of his eye he saw a tear flash down her withered cheek. At the head of the grave there was a large stone marker. The marker was intended for two graves, and had been placed in such a way that when the second grave was dug the stone face would be centered behind both.

"*Mine eyes have seen the glory of the coming of the Lord;*" the Polysirians sang. "*He is trampling out the vintage where the grapes of wrath are stored; HE hath loosed the fearful lightning of his terrible ,swift sword, His truth is marching on.'*"

Nathaniel Drake looked at the marker's stone face. One half of it was blank. On the other half—the half that overlooked the grave-the following letters had been inscribed:

SAINT NATHANIEL DRAKE

Draked knew the answer then and knew what he must do—

What, in a sense, he had done already . . .

He turned to the old woman standing beside him. "When did I first come here?" he asked.

"Fifty-two years ago."

"And how old was I when I died?"

"You were eighty-three."

"Why did I become a saint?"

"You never told me, Nathaniel Drake."

Gently, he touched her cheek. She rased her eyes then, and this time he saw into them—saw the years and the love, and the laughter, the sorrow and the pain. "Were we happy together?" he asked.

"Yes, my darling—thanks to you."

He bent and kissed her upon the forehead. "Good by, Mary Legs," he said, and turned , and walked down the hill.

"*Glory, glory hallelujah,*" the Polysirians sang" as his ship rose up into the sky. "*Glory, glory, hallelujah. Glory, glory hallelujah, his truth is marching on.*"

*

To what may a warp seepage be likened? It may be likened to a leak in the roof of a twentieth-century dwelling. The roofs of century dwellings were supported by rafters, and whenever a leak occurred, the water ran along these rafters and seeped through the ceiling in unexpected places. While the "rafters" of man-made spacewarps are of a far more complex nature than the rafters of such simple dwellings, the basic analogy still holds true: the spatio-

41

temporal elements that escape from space-warps such as the Suez Canal never emerge in the immediate vicinity of the rift.

Even in Nathaniel Drake's day, the, Suez Canal techs knew this, but what they did not know was -that such seepages do not pose a threat to -the continuum, but only to whoever or whatever comes into contact with their foci. Neither did the Suez Canal techs—or anyone else, for that matter-know that the effect of these foci varies in ratio to the directness of the contact, and that in the case of partial contact, the effect upon a human being or an object is seemingly similar to the hypothetical preliminary effect of a Lambda-Xi bombardment. Hence it is not surprising that no one, including Drake himself, had tumbled to the true cause of his "ghosthood": *i.e., that he and the major part of* his *ship, in coming into partial contact with a focus, had been partially transmitted into the past.* Simultaneously, the rest of the ship—and Annabelle Leigh—had come into direct contact with the focus and had been totally transmitted into the past.

Here then was the situation when Drake left Iago Iago:

Part of himself and part of his ship and all of Saint Annabelle Leigh were suspended in a last moment whose temporal location he knew to be somewhere in the year 3614 but, whose location, although he knew it to be within displacement-drive range of Iago Iago, he could only guess at, while the preponderance of himself and the preponderance of his ship hurtled toward the region of space that was responsible for his "ghosthood" and whose co-ordinates he had jotted down in the *Fly by Night's* log over three months ago. In the light of the knowledge with which his visit to Iago Iago had endowed him, he quite naturally assumed that once he and the ship made direct contact with the force that had partially transmitted them, the rest of the transmission would automatically take place—as in a sense it already had. But what Drake did not know, and had no way of knowing, was that spatio-temporal inconsistencies must be balanced before they can be eliminated, and that before total transmission could be effected, his three months-plus sojourn in the future had to be compensated for by a corresponding sojourn in the past, the length of said sojourn to be in inverse ratio to the spatio-temporal distance he would be catapulted. Consequently he was shocked when, following the *Fly by Night's* coincidence with the focus, he emerged, not in the spatio-temporal moment he was prepared for, but in the war-torn skies of a planet of another era and another system.

At the instant of emergence, every warning light on the ship began blinking an angry red, and the scintillometric siren began wailing like an *enfant terrible*. Drake's conditioned reflexes superseded his shock to the extent that he had the anti-fission field activated before the automatic pilot had finished processing the incoming sensoria. Although he did not know it at the time, the shield that the ship threw out cleansed nearly an entire hemisphere of radioactivity and engulfed half an ocean and a whole continent. All of which brings up another aspect of time that was undreamed of in Drake's day: Expansion.

*

Neanderthal man stood knee-high to a twentieth-century grasshopper, and the woolly mammoth that he hunted was no longer than a twentieth-century cicada. The universe expands on a temporal as well as a spatial basis, and this expansion is cumulative. Over a period of half a century, the results are negligible, but when millenia are involved, the results are staggering. Look not to fossils to dispute this seeming paradox, for fossils are an integral part of the planets they are interred upon; and do not point with polemic fingers to such seemingly insuperable obstacles as mass, gravity, and bone tissue, for the cosmos is run on a co-operative basis, and all things both great and small co-operate. Nor are there any discrepancies in the normal order of events. A six-foot man of

a past generation is the equivalent of a six-foot man of a future generation: it is only when you lift them from their respective eras and place them side by side that the difference in relative size becomes manifest. Thus, in the eyes of the inhabitants of the planet he was about to descend upon, Nathaniel Drake would be a figure of heroic proportions, while his ship would loom in the heavens like a small moon—

Or a small planet . . .

Beneath him lay the ruins of a once-magnificent structure. Not far away from the ruins, a pale river ran, and across the river, a city burned brightly in the night. Nathaniel Drake knew where he was then—and when. Looking down upon the ruins, he had an inkling of his destiny. What I do now, he thought, has already been done, and I cannot change it one iota. Therefore, what I do I am destined to do, and I am here to fulfill my destiny.

He still wore his anti-grav belt. He parked the *Fly by Night* on extended jacks, and drifted down to the ground.

Here, cherry trees grew, and the cherry trees were in blossom. Towering above the pink explosions, Nathaniel Drake knew his heroic proportions.

He approached the ruins he had seen from above. The noble columns lay broken; the stately roof had fallen in. The wall, blasphemed not long ago by the hate-steeped scrawls of segregationists, were rivened. Was that a marble hand protruding over there?

A hand. A marble arm. A shattered white-marble leg. Drake knew his destiny then, and began to dig.

No one saw him, for men had become, moles, and cowered in dark places. Above him in the sky, missiles struck the anti-fission shield and winked out like gutted glow-worms. Interceptors blazed up, then blazed back down again, and died. The flames of the burning capital painted the Potomac blood-red.

He continued to dig.

A fallen column lay across the broken marble body. He rolled the column aside. The noble head lay broken on the floor. He picked it up with gentle hands and carried it out and laid it on the spring-damp ground. Piece by piece, he carried the broken statue out, and when he was sure that not a single fragment remained among the ruins, he brought his ship down and loaded the pieces into the hold. Lifting, he set forth for the sea.

Some distance inland from the shores of Chesapeake Bay, he left the ship and drifted down to the bank of the river and began walking, along the river to the sea. Above him, the automatic pilot held the ship on the course.

He felt like a giant, Nathaniel Drake did, walking down the Potomac to the sea, and in this long-ago age a giant he was. But all the while he walked, he knew that compared to the giant he was impersonating, he was a pygmy two feet tall.

. . . and if you cannot believe in the walking of His ghost upon the land and in His ascension to the stars, then you are as one dead, without hope, without love, without pity, without kindness, without humanity, without humility, without sorrow, without pain, without happiness, and without life

"Amen," said Nathaniel Drake.

He came to a village untouched by the destruction around it, and saw people crawling out of underground shelters. Looking down upon them, he proclaimed "Lo, I have arisen. Lo, I walk again! Look at Me, ye peoples of the earth—I have come to emancipate you from your shackling fears, and I have summoned the Planet of Peace from out of the immensities of space and time to transport My ghost to the stars. Lo, I *force* peace upon you, ye peoples of the earth, and I command you to remember always this terrible day when you drove Kindness from your doorsteps and threw wide your portals to Perdition."

On the shore of Chesapeake Bay he halted, and when the automatic pilot brought the ship down, he removed the fragments of the statue from the hold and laid them gently on the beach . . . *And the Planet of Peace absorbed His ghost and bore it from the face of the earth.*

A moment later, complete transmission occurred.

*

The cabin was a lonely place. He left it quickly and hurried down the companionway to the starboard storeroom. The bulkheads no longer shimmered, and the deck was solid beneath his feet. His translucence was no more. He opened the storeroom lock and stepped across the threshold. Mary Legs, nee Annabelle Leigh, was huddled on the floor. She looked up when she heard his step, and in her eyes was the dumb and hopeless misery of an animal that is cornered and does not now what to do.

He raised her gently to her feet. "Next stop, Iago Iago," he said.